Animal Adventures
at Rainbow Cottage

Betty Salthouse

With illustrations by

Martha Frankland

Best wishes,

Betty Salthouse

ANIMAL ADVENTURES
AT RAINBOW COTTAGE
© Copyright Betty Salthouse 2018
All rights reserved
Published by Hawkesbury Press 2018
www.hawkesburypress.com
ISBN10 1911223275
ISBN13 9781911223276
Also available as an ebook

Illustrations by Martha Frankland
Interior design by Debbie Young
Proofread by Zedolus Proofreading and
Author Services

This work is a piece of fiction. Any similarity to real people or places is purely coincidental.
A CIP catalogue record for this book is available from the British Library.

To my family

Chapter 1

Spring Comes to Rainbow Cottage

Sidney Spider stretched his long legs in the deepest, darkest cupboard where he had spent the winter. All the noise of things being moved around had woken him up, so it must be time for him to be up and about.

He had spent several winters in the cottage, dozing mostly because it was so cosy and warm. Mrs Green pretended he wasn't there, because she had seen him scuttle away when she had moved a heavy pot, but she was always careful not to knock or squeeze him. She would never harm a living thing if she could help it.

Now all was hustle and bustle, because spring had arrived. What a busy time it was. Mrs Green didn't mind the bright sunshine showing up the dirty marks on the fireside chair, or the dust that had crept into the corners of the window ledges, because she was pleased to be reminded that it was special cleaning time again. She loved spring cleaning, and she loved the spring.

But Sidney Spider wasn't used to the strong light when he first poked his head out of the cupboard, and so he decided to make his way into the garden very slowly.

First, he stopped behind the kitchen dresser, on which stood all the blue and white crockery.

Then he rested behind the coal scuttle which now lay empty.

Finally, he took a short nap in the leaves of the big fern plant that grew in a brown pot in the corner, before scuttling through the door and round the side of the cottage to the woodshed. There was no sign of Spots the dog, who liked to lie with his head on his paws and one eye open.

Gosh, it is sunny! Sidney thought as he climbed up under the tiles on the roof. So he waited for his eight eyes to get used to the sunshine before looking around at the garden.

Then he saw a lovely sight. The daffodils were nodding their yellow heads in banks of colour, and there were bright green shoots popping up everywhere. When he had crawled through the damp leaves of autumn it had been a very different picture. Then he had been bumped on the head by falling leaves. Spring was definitely safer!

It was great to be out and about. Soon he would go and see his friends, and then find his favourite place in the plum tree.

Meanwhile, Mrs Green had laid out lots of old newspapers on the large flagstones at the back of the cottage. She was now putting everything from the cupboards in rows, checking if any handles needed tightening, or if anything was chipped or cracked. If it was, she would use it for something else, perhaps for storing bits and pieces. She didn't like throwing anything away, ever!

Mrs Green had lived in Rainbow Cottage for a very long time, and it was difficult for her to remember living anywhere else. She had called it Rainbow Cottage because it was her pot of gold at the end of the rainbow, and she couldn't have been happier. All the animals that lived there were pleased to call it home.

Chapter 2

The Visit

It was such a nice day that William Woodlouse decided to get up early. He asked his mother if he could go for a walk and visit Sam Snail, who lived in the garden wall. Mrs Woodlouse said he could, as long as he was back before the sun rose too high in the sky. She didn't want him to get sun-dried, or he would be very uncomfortable.

7

So William left his home in the woodpile and set out. Sam Snail always told him lots of stories about what used to happen in the garden long ago, right back to the time when he was a youngster. Sam knew more about history than any other animal that lived there, and William always enjoyed going to see him. He was the last of several generations of snails to live in the old stone wall.

Once upon a time, there had been mothers and fathers, grandmothers and grandfathers, brothers and sisters, uncles and aunts, and lots and lots of cousins as well. But over the years the rest of the family had either moved away or died - leaving only old Sam. But Sam was never lonely, because often one of his relatives came to visit. Sam lived near the bottom of the wall, behind one of the large flat stones which served as a porch.

"Morning, Mr Sam," said William, when he saw him sitting in the doorway studying the weather, as was his custom. "How are you today?"

"Well, I feel a bit chesty and I've got a cough," he said. "But now that spring is here, with something fresh to eat, I expect I will soon be right as rain.

Come, in young William, and sit yourself down."

As soon as William was settled in a nice comfy corner of Sam's house, he told him about the day the snails had crawled all the way to Waterley Bottom for a picnic. It had turned out to be the best picnic anyone could ever remember. When it was time to come home some snails had eaten so much they could scarcely crawl, and had to be rolled home.

"You should have seen them going down the hills," said Sam, and he threw back his head and laughed and laughed, until his eyes watered with the memory of it.

Sam Snail always gave William some tit-bit he had been keeping for him, and today it was a tiny new shoot from one of the weeds that grew in the garden. Sam only ate the weeds, and not the plants that were grown by Mrs Green, but he never went hungry.

Soon after saying goodbye to Sam, William was practising his climbing skills on the rockery. He wanted one day to be strong enough to climb Giant's Rock, which was a well-known landmark several fields and woods away. Sam had told him that once a famous woodlouse called Fearless Fred had done just that.

At the bottom of the rockery was the garden pond, which was in the shade of the plum tree. By now the sun was much warmer and his skin was beginning to feel a bit dry, but instead of crawling under something damp for a while, he decided it would be much more fun to dangle his legs in the pond.

He had just climbed on top of a very large stone at the edge, when he lost his balance and fell – splash! – into the water. Down and down, he went. Then he bobbed up to the surface, on his back with his legs thrashing the air.

"Glug-glug-glug," he gasped. "I think I'm drowning!"

He felt his legs and tummy warming in the sun, and shouted "HELP!" in his loudest voice. The water was moving under a gentle breeze, and he began drifting out into the middle of the pond, as his voice grew weaker.

Suddenly a twig fell from the plum tree above, and set up an enormous wave which swept him over onto his tummy. He tried to swim, but his legs got all mixed up and he began to cry. Then, overhead, came a shout. It was Sidney Spider.

"Hold on, William, I'm coming!" he called. "Don't panic, I'll rescue you!"

Then he lowered himself swiftly on a strong silken thread. By now poor William was nearly exhausted and had sunk much further in the water.

Sidney stretched out a leg, and then another, and another, until he was able to drag William dripping from the pond. He held him above the water until William felt strong enough to begin the difficult climb back up the long silken thread to the safety of the plum tree above.

It was the hardest thing that Sidney Spider had ever done. He wasn't even

14

sure the thread would hold both of them, but slowly they rose higher and higher. Sidney was very glad he had eight legs. He knew he couldn't have managed with less, but it seemed a very long time before he was able to scramble onto a branch of the plum tree.

He laid William flat on his back and blew gently on his face, because poor William seemed to have passed out with shock.

"Where am I?" William gasped, when the rush of air made him open his eyes.

"It's all right now," said Sidney. "I've rescued you, and you're safe in the plum tree."

"Oh dear, what a silly woodlouse I am," he said. "I just wanted to dangle my legs in the water, and then I fell in. I think I'm the wrong shape to paddle." He closed his eyes with exhaustion.

"Never mind," said Sidney. "You're all right now. When you have recovered, you can go home and tell your family about your adventure."

"I don't think I will tell anyone," mumbled William, opening one eye. "It was more of an accident than an adventure, and I don't want anyone to

16

know how silly I am. And thank you Sidney, for being so brave. I shall never forget it."

And he never did.

Chapter 3

Sam Snail Hears

Some Disturbing News

At the side of Rainbow Cottage was a rose garden, and in the corner was a wooden seat under an arch of trailing roses. This is where Mrs Green liked to sit and enjoy the garden. It was a place where she liked to do her knitting and sewing, or sometimes read a book or write a letter. When the roses were out, which was usually from June onwards, she could daydream in the scented air from the velvety flowers. It was such a pretty place that Sarah Slug had decided to set up home there.

One day Mrs Green was sitting waiting for Mr Bill, the Odd Job Man, to come. Mrs Green was finishing a sleeve of a forget-me-not blue jumper she was knitting, when Sarah Slug overheard Mrs Green say to herself: "Perhaps a fence might be better than a wall."

When Sarah heard these words, she immediately thought of poor Sam Snail and his home in the wall. She must quickly tell him the news!

So, as Mrs Green gathered up her knitting to go back into the cottage, Sarah picked up her freshest parasol, made from a dock leaf, and set off to the drystone wall. She always carried a leaf parasol to protect her from the sun or rain, or any nosy-parker bird she might meet. As Mrs Green went one way, Sarah went another.

When Sarah passed the herbaceous border, she thought: *What a funny name for a flower bed!* Then she saw Buster Bee, who was there gathering dusty-yellow pollen from the tulips, and she would have liked to stop for a chat. Instead, she called: "Can't stop now! Urgent business."

She tried to hurry past the rockery and garden pond, but her parasol felt very heavy today. It was one of her largest. When she reached the wall, she called out "Ooo-ee! Sam." Then as he came to the door, her words tumbled out: "It's going to come down!"

"What is?" asked Sam Snail, taken completely by surprise, and with his wits still scrambled from a good night's sleep.

"The wall of course," gushed Sarah. She didn't mean to be pushy or rude, but sometimes she was so excited at being the carrier of really important news, she couldn't help it.

"Well, well, well, I never," said Sam. "And which wall would this be?"

"Your wall of course, you silly billy," she said. The thought that it might be another wall hadn't entered her head.

"Oh dear, I hope not," said Sam. "I'm much too old to move. How do you know?"

"Only this morning I heard Mrs Green say that a fence might be better than a wall, and I think Mr Bill is coming to see about it," said Sarah.

"That is a pity," said Sam. "I don't know where else I could live."

"You could go and live under a flower pot," said Sarah.

"I don't think a flower pot is a good idea," said Sam. "It might be picked up and used for potting anytime."

A flower pot indeed! What security would he have under a flower pot? Although Sarah was a good friend of his, he often felt a bit browbeaten by her.

"What about the rhubarb patch by the stream?" she suggested. "Lots of snails live there already."

"I know, and I'm not a snob, but I'd like something a bit more permanent than a rhubarb patch," he said. "I have been used to a very good address."

"Well, I'm sorry to bring you the bad news, but I wanted you to be the first to know," she said. "Sorry I can't stay any longer now, but I hope you'll find somewhere else to live when the time comes."

And off she crawled, with her parasol high in the air.

Sam watched her go, feeling just a bit sorry for himself. He was too old to move, and life with all those boisterous young snails didn't bear thinking about. He wanted peace and quiet at his time of life. He couldn't imagine Mrs Green doing such a thing. To pull the wall down seemed preposterous. That really was a big word for a snail to use, but it was the best one he could think of. It was such a beautiful wall, built from lovely creamy stone and spangled with brown and yellow lichens, while through its crevices tumbled bright stars of yellow stonecrop.

"I suppose I am an old stick-in-the-mud," mumbled Sam, as he crawled away to sort out a few things, in case he had to move in a hurry. He knew that many animals had to move suddenly without any warning. He had heard of other places where noisy machines had moved in and dug up all the gardens, throwing animals out of house and home. At least he had been warned!

Later that day, Sam was disturbed by the sound of voices. It was Mrs Green talking to Mr Bill.

"I was thinking of having a fence, or maybe a wall to hide the compost heap and the woodpile. What do you think,

Mr Bill? This part of the garden is a bit of a muddle."

"No need for a wall, and more expense too," said Mr Bill. "I could put up a bit of a fence, or you could plant a nice big rhododendron in front. That would do the trick!"

"Well, thank you for your good advice, Mr Bill," said Mrs Green. "A nice rhododendron sounds lovely. I think I will chose a pretty pink colour, it's my favourite."

That was it! Sam Snail felt all topsy-turvy with happiness. Sarah the silly slug had got it all wrong. It wasn't "his" wall they were talking about. He wouldn't have to move after all.

Now it was his turn to go visiting. He couldn't wait to tell her!

Chapter 4

Martin Millipede

Has a Problem

In the rose garden, Sarah Slug gave lessons to young animals when she wasn't too busy doing other things. Then she sent Flitter and Flutter

Butterfly, her young neighbours, to tell everyone to come. Because school only happened sometimes, it was called "The Miss Sarah Slug Sometimes School for Young Animals".

Sarah tried to make sure that everyone in the garden was brought up properly with good manners, and to have respect for their parents. All the mums and dads thought Sarah did a very good job. She was a very clever slug, and liked to teach any youngster who was keen to learn. One of her brightest pupils was Anthony Ant. He loved doing number work, and usually got all his answers right.

Right now, Sarah had just finished making a new parasol from a fine dock leaf, and had stood it in water to keep fresh until she needed it. Her spring-cleaning was done too, even before Mrs Green's, and in front of her she could see a clear day, so she decided to ask Flitter and Flutter to fly off and tell everyone it was school today!

First, they flew to William Woodlouse's house in the woodpile, and then to Anthony Ant's house under the garden path. Anthony's mother said he must put his muddles away before he went anywhere. Anthony was always making things, or finding out how they worked, and today he was building a lift from a piece of stick and string he'd found.

Soon Flitter and Flutter had made all their calls and went back to tell Miss Sarah, who was still in the middle of getting things ready. She found it quite difficult to mix clay into paint without the help of Sidney Spider, who often came along to help with jobs, but today there was no sign of him. He usually called in on his early morning swing round the garden, and had lots of silken swings he used daily to keep fit. Now and again Sam Snail came along to talk about the past, because he was an expert on History.

Soon everyone started to arrive, but when Martin Millipede came, he was very upset.

"Whatever is the matter, Martin?" asked Sarah, giving him a motherly hug. She didn't like to see anyone unhappy for long.

Martin sniffed loudly, and said the snails in the rhubarb patch had been calling him names, because he didn't know how many legs he had.

"Oh dear, we must do something about that," said Miss Sarah. After calling the register she told them to make footprint paintings, so they could count them.

"You can use red and yellow paint that I've mixed with fresh rainwater," she said.

Soon they were all busy having great fun, walking about with wet feet on the big flat stones between the bushes.

"Look!" called Flitter Butterfly, who had finished hers and was flying around watching the others. "Martin's got lots more than anyone else, even more than William."

"I know, and it's very hard to count high numbers," said Martin, remembering being teased.

36

When they had all finished, Sarah asked Anthony Ant if he would help with the counting.

"Please can we start with mine?" asked Lenny Ladybird. "'Cause I haven't got many."

"That's a good idea," said Sarah. So they all counted up to six, with Anthony counting the loudest. Then Sarah reminded them that all insects have six legs.

William's turn was next. He had made lots of smudges, but they managed to get up to twenty-two. Then Sarah wrote in a silvery trail on her special board.

"Now it's Martin's turn," she said. "And then there will be no more teasing. Come on Anthony, you can start counting."

Sarah was very cross that the young snails didn't come to school often enough, and were picking up all sorts of bad habits.

Anthony hadn't counted to such a high number before, but he got up to one hundred and fifteen on one side without any help from the teacher. Then they counted the rest together, and it came to two hundred and thirty. Sarah wrote it thickly in silver, and told Martin to learn it off by heart.

Soon it was playtime, and Sarah said they could all have extra play for working so hard. So off they all went to the play area, where there were all sorts of things to crawl over and jump on, while the butterflies practiced their take-offs and landings. Everybody could hear Martin Millipede saying he had two hundred and thirty legs, which was more than anyone else. Lucy Ladybird said she thought he was boasting, which was just as bad as teasing, and he shouldn't do it.

But Martin didn't mind her scolding, because now he really did know how many legs he had.

Chapter 5

The Sand Pile

William Woodlouse and Anthony Ant were walking past a pile of sand that the builders had left behind, when they saw Black Beetle foraging about on the top. Suddenly the sand started to move, and she came tumbling down to the bottom.

"That looks fun," said Anthony Ant to William. "Perhaps we could make a slide".

41

"I don't think we shall have to make one," said William. "If we can climb to the top, I think we will come down very fast."

The sand was dry and moved easily. Black Beetle had landed on it to eat a tasty titbit that she'd noticed while flying by, and had found herself going helter-skelter down to the bottom. The sand was piled against the kitchen wall, where it had been used for alterations inside the cottage.

There was no one about, because Mrs Green and Spots the dog had gone to collect the eggs and milk from Farmer Wellington's at Green Valley

Farm, so William and Anthony crawled up the wall and onto the top of the pile of sand. Then they slid down again, helter-skelter to the bottom. It was great fun, and they were making so much noise that Sarah Slug heard them from the rose garden, and came across to see what was going on.

"And what are you two youngsters up to?" she asked.

"We're having sand-slides!" they chorused. "Why don't you come up and join us, Miss Sarah? It's great fun!"

"I can see that," she smiled. "Perhaps I will, if no one is looking."

So, after looking around to make sure no one was in sight, she put down her parasol and crawled up the wall.

"You do it like this," said Anthony, holding his legs in the air and zooming down to the bottom with a loud shriek.

"All right," said Sarah," I will try."

She wiggled herself into a sitting position. But she didn't feel quite right.

"Curl up tight and roll down," suggested William, wanting her to have as much fun as they were having.

So that's what Sarah did. After taking a dizzy tumble, she found herself in a messy heap at the bottom, sand sticking to her like glue. She felt a very silly slug indeed! Thank goodness Sam Snail couldn't see her like this, all covered in grit.

"Are you all right, Miss Sarah?" called William and Anthony from the top of the pile, ready for the next go. But before Sarah could find enough breath to answer, around the corner came Sam Snail, leaning heavily on his walking stick.

"Goodness me, Miss Sarah. Whatever have you been doing?"

"I've been having fun," Sarah said, with a sniff. "I'm not an old stick-in-the-mud!"

And off she went, to find some wet grass to crawl into.

It was a long time since Sam had seen Sarah playing such games, and he had a little chuckle.

"Leave it to the youngsters," he said to himself, as he went on his way.

Meanwhile, Anthony and William played on the slide until they were both very tired, and rather dirty. Then they went home for dinner. But next day when they went back to play again, they found the sand all wet and sticky because it had been raining. Then they remembered Miss Sarah and couldn't help chuckling too!

Chapter 6

Wally Worm Sees
the Other World

Wally Worm was very excited, because he was making his own tunnel for the very first time, although he had practised lots of times before with his mother. He pushed and stretched and pushed and stretched, until he felt exhausted. It was hard work, but the tunnel had soon grown quite long. Some of the soil he spat out, and some went right through his tummy, but he didn't mind, because worms have to get used to that.

Suddenly, he came to a big stone. He would have to go around it. But which way was best? *I think it will be quicker if I go over it,* he thought. As he pushed up and over the stone, he had a funny feeling that he might be near the Other World which lay above the ground, but he had to go on. He couldn't stop now! His mother had warned him about the

Other World. "It's a world with lights, where danger sees you," she had told him. He had also heard exciting stories about it from Black Beetle, who came into the tunnel on visits.

Then he felt a rush of fresh air, and saw a bright shiny thing looking down at him. Wally didn't know it, but this was the sun shining down from a bright blue sky, and he had come up at the side of the cabbage patch. He felt the warm sun on his back for the very first time, before a strange shadow crossed over him.

He cowered under a large leaf, remembering his mother's warning: "If you ever find yourself in the Other World, watch out for birds, because they are our greatest enemy." He remembered how his Uncle Fred had been pulled from his burrow by a big blackbird, when he had chanced to put out his head to see if it was going to rain. It hadn't rained for weeks and weeks, and the tunnels were dry and dusty.

Wally waited, but the dark shadow didn't come back. His heart was beating so loud that if anybody had been there they would have heard it.

And then a gruff voice said: "Hello, I'm Sam Snail; and who are you?"

"Goodness me, you made me jump!" squeaked Wally, feeling very panicky. When he had recovered, he said: "My name is Wally."

"Pleased to meet you," said Sam. "Out for a breather, I suppose? Couldn't stand the underground life myself. Still, what suits one doesn't suit another, and it wouldn't do if it did."

"Well, I want to be here, and yet I don't," mumbled Wally. "If you know what I mean."

It sounded a bit muddled to Sam, but he wanted to be polite, so he just nodded his head.

"It is exciting being somewhere really different and dangerous," said Wally. "But I know I shouldn't be here."

"If you stay for a bit, I could show you round," said Sam. "I'll take care of you."

As Wally had never met a snail before he was very pleased, and off they went together. As they went across the path, poor Wally felt the rough stone scratch his tummy, but afterwards he enjoyed a lovely wriggle through the lawn.

Sam showed Wally where he lived in the wall, and then they passed a puddle.

"What's that?" asked Wally.

"That's a puddle," replied Sam. "You'd better be careful of those, Wally."

Sam had often seen relatives of Wally's lying in the bottom of puddles after the rain, but he didn't tell Wally that.

Wally was now beginning to get quite tired. It was much easier to wriggle through a tunnel than along the ground, he discovered, and he knew his mother would be getting worried if she couldn't find him.

"Can we go back to the cabbage patch?" he asked. "I think it's time I went home."

They soon found the entrance to Wally's burrow, but Sam was sorry to see his new friend go.

"Goodbye, Sam," said Wally. "Thank you, and see you again sometime."

And then he disappeared into his dark tunnel.

Sam crawled away, feeling happy and sad, and knowing what Wally had meant.

Chapter 7

Sidney Spider's Busy Day

"Ho-ho-ho!

Hee-hee-hee!

I'm as happy as can be!"

Sidney Spider sang from high in the plum tree. Well, almost as happy as can be, he thought. He was enjoying summer in the garden among the green leaves of the plum tree, but how nice it would be to share it with another spider. Perhaps even a wife?

"I'll spin a new web, a really special web," he said to himself. "Then perhaps someone will come."

So he began spinning, up and down then round and round. First he laid out the spokes so they looked like big sunbeams of shiny silk, and then he joined them up very carefully.

"Oh, this is rather fun!
A spider's work is never done!"

He sang because he was really enjoying his work today. But there were a lot more rounds and rounds than up and downs, and he was feeling just a bit dizzy by the time he had finished it. But it was a lovely web, and he was very pleased with it.

Even the Queen of Spiders would like to live in this, he thought to himself. *And now I will sing a song to say it's ready!*

So he sang:

"I live all alone in my nice little home,
Tra-la-la-la-dee!
Please, oh please, will someone join me!
Tra-la-la-la-dee!"

At first he sang it high, so the notes floated across the garden and over the trees in the orchard. Then he sang it low, so the notes tumbled down and reached the hidden places deep in the ferns and tall grasses.

Then, overhead came a whirling sound, like a little helicopter. It was Lucy Ladybird.

"What's the matter, Sidney?" she called down. "Was that a cry for help?"

"Cry for help indeed, certainly not!" said Sidney, feeling a little offended. Then he told Lucy how he had made a special new web, and about his wish to share it. So Lucy sat on a leaf and puzzled about how she could help him.

"Perhaps you could sing a song, Sidney, about what you like doing best. Then anyone listening will know something about you."

"That sounds a good idea, Lucy," he said.

"What do you really like doing best?" she asked.

"Eating strawberry jam," said Sidney. "But I have only eaten it once, when Mrs Green left a jam tart on a plate in the garden. It was del-ic-ious. Absolutely delicious!"

"Well, why don't you sing:

59

"I'm a very happy spider,
Oh yes I am,
Especially when I'm eating
strawberry jam!"

"I will try anything once," said Sidney. "Thank you so much, Lucy."

"Goodbye, and good luck!" she called, and off she flew.

Sidney liked singing about strawberry jam. It reminded him of the delicious taste, and he wished very much he had some more to eat.

Then, suddenly, he heard a soft voice say:

"I love it too."

He turned around, and there peeping over the side of the web was a very shy lady spider.

"Please do come up," said Sidney "It's so nice of you to come," said Sidney. "Do you really like strawberry jam?"

"Yes," she said. "And when the strawberries are ripe, I make a little myself."

"Gosh, do you?" Sidney couldn't believe his ears. "Well, I'm Sidney," he said, holding out a welcoming leg.

"I'm Miranda," she whispered. "And I did enjoy your song. Please could you sing it again?"

"Then I'll sing it just for you," said Sidney, as they both sat down together.

Now Sidney was really happy!

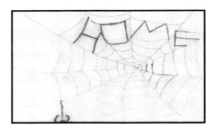

Chapter 8

Celebrations

The garden was a-buzz with the news. There was going to be a Summer Fair, with sports and races and lots of other exciting things. Mrs Green was going to spend a week's holiday with her sister, so it was the best time for the animals to have it. They could invite friends and relations from far and wide, and have super celebrations!

The date had been quickly set, as soon as Sarah Slug had heard the news that Mrs Green was planning to leave the following Friday, to travel to Golden-Beach-On-Sea. The Summer Fair would be held on the Saturday following her departure.

Sarah Slug had formed a committee to help her get things ready, and this consisted of Sam Snail, Mrs Woodlouse Senior, and Sidney Spider. Sarah would be in charge of the organisation, because she was good at writing lists. They were going to hold it in a large clearing in the orchard under the apple trees.

Soon all the work of getting the Summer Fair ready had been shared out. Sam Snail was keen to run the sports, and was going to ask all the animals which were their favourite races so they could have a good selection. Mrs Woodlouse Senior was going to do the food, and would make sure that no-one went hungry. Sidney Spider was going to put up a large tent with the help of the Ant family, which could be used as a meeting place to serve the food.

Soon Sarah had drawn up a list of animals to be sent an invitation, and had asked Flitter and Flutter Butterfly to deliver them. After Mrs Green had packed her blue suitcase and gone in Farmer Wellington's car to the station, the great day finally dawned.

Sam Snail, who was always up bright and early, was down in the orchard tracking out the start and finish lines for the races, when Sarah Slug arrived.

"It's an early snail that marks a trail," she smiled, always keen to bring a bit of poetry into the conversation.

"Yes, and I think that'll do," Sam said smugly, pleased to have made the first move of the day.

"I will wait inside the tent and check my notes," said Sarah, and off she crawled under the hanging flap.

Sidney Spider and the Ants had used several large rhubarb leaves to build the tent, which Sidney had secured firmly together with extra strong silk. Inside the tent it would stay fresh and cool, and there was a nice large space for everyone to gather in for the announcements.

"Morning Sam," said Sidney Spider when he arrived. "I'm going to spin some bunting."

"That will be nice," said Sam, remembering other grand occasions. "I like to see the flags flying."

Sidney Spider had brought along some pretty paper he'd collected from the hedgerows. He didn't like to see messy hedgerows so he often picked it up, and sometimes it came in useful, like today. Mrs Green would have called it recycling. Soon colourful flags were fluttering above the entrance to the orchard.

Then Mrs Woodlouse Senior came and began seeing to the food, and it wasn't long before other animals began arriving in dribs and drabs.

Then came a shout from William Woodlouse, who had spotted Sam's family straggling through the gate; Sam waved a greeting to them, and said he'd see them in a minute.

Soon there were little groups of animals all over the orchard, chattering away nineteen to the dozen. *It's time to get everyone together,* thought Sarah Slug as she poked her head out from under the tent flap. They had not decided on a firm starting time, but were going to begin when a good number had arrived.

Then Sarah waved her parasol at Sam Snail, which was the signal for everyone to come into the tent. He passed the message round, and soon everyone began arranging themselves inside.

Sarah stood high on a very large stone at one end, and when everyone had settled, she began.

"I am pleased to welcome you all to our Grand Summer Fair. I do hope everyone has a super time, and I want to thank all those who helped to get it ready, especially…"

Then, as she gave out a long list of names, some animals started to fidget.

"Let's have one big cheer and we'll begin," she said. "But don't forget, I'd like a few volunteers to stay behind at the end to help clear up. We must leave the orchard as we found it."

At this point, lots of hands shot up in the air, and Sarah hoped they would remember. Then, as the cheering died away, everyone scrambled outside to begin.

"Over here for the Snails' Crawl!" shouted Sam. He thought he would start with that because it always took a long time. Then everyone else could have a wander about if they didn't want to watch.

Soon, those taking part were lined up. Sam shouted "GO!" while Sarah waved her parasol as a starting flag, and they were off. Everyone watched as the young snails from the rhubarb patch took the lead, with the ones who had been teasing Martin Millipede in front. Martin secretly wished none of them would win.

As they came to the finish, Sidney Spider announced from his seat in the apple tree over the finishing line that the winner was Miss Suzy Snail. As she was well liked, everyone cheered loudly.

This was followed by a flying race, but unfortunately there had to be a re-fly because Buster Bee had bumped into Lucy Ladybird, who had been put off balance and was now crying.

Then Sarah Slug got very cross with some young snails who were arguing about the result of the snail race, saying it wasn't fair because the ground on which Suzy Snail had crawled was much smoother and that's why she had won. But when they heard that lollipops were being given out on the lollipop stall, they all rushed off to get one and forgot about the result of the race.

After that, all the races were run without any problems, and everyone had great fun!

There was an old'uns race as well as a young'uns race, then a walking backwards race, which the woodlice did particularly well in, and a many-legged race which was Martin Millipede's favourite.

Soon it was time for cool drinks and a rest, so while the youngsters stayed outside to play, the grown-ups went inside the tent for a natter. Then there was a special show in a ring, with acrobatics, juggling, dancing, and all manner of things. While all this was going on, Mrs Woodlouse Senior was serving snacks in the big tent.

Then came the time for tired animals to say goodbye and start the trek home, but those who had travelled a long way were staying with families in the garden.

Sam Snail's wall was going to be very crowded because so many of his relations had come, but he was looking forward to having a good chin-wag about the old days.

Then it was time for Sidney Spider to take down the bunting and store it away. Sarah Slug was glad so many had stayed behind to help, and gave everyone clearing up jobs to do.

There was a big shout of "Everybody clear!" when the big tent finally came down, and that was the end of a lovely day. Soon the orchard had settled down to a peaceful night under a silver moon. As Sarah prepared for bed, she hoped Mrs Green would have as much fun as they'd had today!

Chapter 9

George Grasshopper
Looks for a Home

George Grasshopper was a shy young grasshopper, who was very big for his age. He lived with his parents and brothers and sisters at the edge of Long Meadow.

One day, his father said: "George, don't you think it's time you found a home of your own? We are finding it a bit of a squash all living in the same house. And one day you might want to have a family of your own."

George knew his father was right, so one day he decided to be brave, and, after saying goodbye to his parents, he set out with only a few belongings on his back, tied up in his favourite handkerchief.

He jumped along looking for somewhere nice, but every now and then he stopped to practice a Hello Song, that he made by rubbing his back legs against his wings. And it sounded like this, "Rick-a-tick! Rick-a-tack! Zick-a-zick! Zick-a-zack!", which in grasshopper language means, "Hello I'm pleased to meet you." He was going to sing his song when he found a new home, and then he hoped he would soon make friends. He knew he would miss his parents, and he didn't want to be lonely for very long.

After a little while, he came to the river bank and landed on a tall grass stalk. As it looked a nice place, he began to sing his new song. He had just got as far as rick-a-tick, rick-a-tack, when up popped a head over a dandelion flower.

It was Johnny Cricket, a distant relative of George's.

"Hello," said George, when he saw Johnny. "This looks a very pretty place. I thought it might make a nice home for me."

"That's what everybody thinks!" said Johnny crossly. "That's why it's so overcrowded. I can't take three hops without landing on somebody! I think if anyone else comes to live here, we will all end up falling in the river."

"Oh dear," said George, not wanting to upset anyone. "I think I had better be on my way then, and try somewhere else."

"I don't want to be a wet blanket, but that does seem a good idea," chirped the cricket, and off he hopped, leaving George just a little bit crestfallen.

Never mind, he thought, perhaps the next place I find will be even nicer. So off he went to try again.

He bounded merrily along because it was such a lovely day, and very soon he passed a field full of big black and white cows, all busy tearing off huge bunches of grass with their long, rasping tongues. *Not a good place to live,* he thought. *I might get eaten up.*

Then he came to a field behind the orchard at Green Valley Farm. It did seem a nice place, so he landed on a grassy mound and sat down to sing his Hello Song, but he had only got as far as, "Rick-a- ," when a Beetle came along.

"Hello," said George to the beetle. "I am looking for a new home, and I was hoping this would be suitable."

"Please yourself," replied the beetle, stopping to clean its wings. "But I wouldn't want to live here. What with the hens and the goats, I shouldn't think you would be very happy here at all."

"Oh dear, won't I?" said George, wondering if he would ever find the right place. "Will the hens and goats be any bother?"

"Of course they will," replied the beetle. "The hens come out here from the farm for a good scratch, and of course the goats don't care where they step. I nearly lost my back leg yesterday, and I'm only here on a visit. You see, once upon a time this used to be my home, but times have changed, and I wouldn't want to live here anymore."

Buster Bee was just drinking nectar from a purple clover flower when he heard the conversation.

"I hope you don't mind me interrupting, but I couldn't help overhearing what you were saying, and I think I know just the place," he said.

"Do you?" said George, feeling happier. "Where is that?"

"Well, I live in a garden," said Buster. "It's a very friendly garden, and we are all very happy there. I'm sure you would be welcome too. If you follow me, I will show you the way; I'll fly ahead very slowly. It's down the lane."

So George said goodbye to the beetle, and off they went. It wasn't long before they arrived at Rainbow Cottage.

"This way," said Buster. "I'll take you to see Sarah Slug first of all. She likes to know all the news."

Sarah was very pleased to see George, because she said he would be the first grasshopper to live in the garden for a long time. Then they went to see Sam Snail in the garden wall. Sam said the cottage garden had suited him for all these years, so he thought George might be happy too.

Then they went to see William Woodlouse, who suggested that George might like to live in the grassy bank at the bottom of the garden. So off they all went to help him settle in. George found a nice cosy home near a lilac tree, and it wasn't long before he was ready to say "Hello" to the rest of his neighbours. He sat down and sang, "Rick-a-tick! Rick-a-tack! Zick-a-zick! Zick-a-zack!" as loud as he could.

Soon all the ants arrived, and then the woodlice, and it wasn't long before everybody was there to say how pleased they were to meet him. What a happy grasshopper George was, now that he had found a new home and lots of friends.

That night, George went to bed tired but happy. One day he would go back to tell his Mum and Dad about his new home. With that happy thought, he closed his eyes and went to sleep.

Anthony Ant Goes
to the Flower Show

Anthony Ant was minding his own
business and having a nice, quiet doze in
the smiling face of a pansy flower, when
he was suddenly woken by a hand
reaching out to pick it. Then he was

hoisted through the air to join some other pansies in a bunch.

Mrs Green had told Susan, a little girl who lived in the lane, that she could pick some flowers to put in a little garden she was making for the Flower Show at the Village Hall. It was a garden on a plate.

Susan took the bunch of pansies she had picked into the kitchen of Rainbow Cottage to show Mrs Green, unaware of Anthony still sitting on one of the flowers. Then Anthony found himself having a ride down the lane to Blackberry Cottage, where Susan lived.

He tried to hide while Susan finished making her garden, which was on a large blue and white oval plate that she had lined with soil and covered with moss. There was a little pebble path with a tiny mirror for a pond, and the pansies were poked in round the edge of the plate to make a pretty border. Anthony clung on for dear life when it was the turn of the pansy flower he was sitting on to be poked in. He hoped he wouldn't be noticed, but Susan was thinking about how nice the little garden looked with the soft, velvety pansy flowers.

Then it was finished, and very soon Anthony found himself being carried off down the lane again, this time to the Village Hall. There Susan's garden was put with lots of other little gardens on a big white tablecloth, next to some vases of colourful dahlias that looked very proud of themselves. He wondered what would happen next, and if anyone had missed him at home. Perhaps they'd sent out a search party. But no-one had noticed that he was gone, and his mother was busying sorting away spare food for times when food was scarce.

The big room at the Village Hall was full of bright flowers and fresh fruit and vegetables. There were pots of jams and honey, all with neat little labels, and lots of bottles of wine, in lovely shades of pale pink and purple, some so clear that he could see through to the other side. There were all sorts of things from people's gardens and from wild places as well.

Soon it was time for the judging, and when the vicar came around with Farmer Wellington, he poked a finger in Susan's dish to see if the pond was real. Anthony was most surprised. Then, later on, a red card was slipped under the corner, on which was written some very large letters and a number one. Susan sounded pleased when she saw it, and Anthony felt sure she had done well.

Then the show opened to the public, and so many people came that it got very hot. Lots of windows were opened and when Anthony looked up, he saw that Buster Bee had flown in.

He was just about to shout, "Rescue me please!" when people started flapping Buster to go out. Not liking to be where he wasn't wanted, he soon went!

Shortly afterwards, Lucy Ladybird walked up the window pane near the little garden, but she didn't seem to see him.

It must be the lovely smells that are telling them to come, he thought.

Soon afterwards, people started moving things around, and his plate was picked up and carried outside. By now he was feeling very homesick, and wanted very much to see Rainbow Cottage again. He could try to walk home, but he wasn't quite brave enough to try.

Meanwhile, Susan was so pleased that she had won first prize that she decided to give her garden to Mrs Green, so Anthony found himself once more at Rainbow Cottage, this time sitting on the window sill. And when the window was opened to let in some fresh air, he made his escape, back to his home under the garden path.

His mother was most surprised when he told her about his adventure, and next day he proudly told William Woodlouse. William said that something like that had once happened to him, when he had been "collected" and taken on a visit to the school. There he had been peered at through a big glass eye, and some children had drawn pictures of him that looked rather good. Luckily, afterwards he had returned to the woodpile, but he didn't want the experience to be repeated. He could easily have been squashed, although he said Susan had been very kind.

"All's well that ends well," said Mrs Ant, as she kissed Anthony goodnight at bedtime. "Life can be full of surprises."

That night, Anthony dreamt he was sitting in a cherry blossom when along came a big wind and blew him around the world. And it was fun!

Chapter 11

Preparations for Winter

It had been a lovely summer, but all good things must come to an end. Now it was autumn, and the nights were drawing in. Busy animals everywhere were doing last minute jobs in preparation for the long dark days ahead, and winter was just around the corner.

Soon, Flitter and Flutter Butterfly would say goodbye, and spend the winter hiding somewhere warm and dry, where icy winds and freezing frosts wouldn't reach them. Up on a wooden beam in the back-bedroom of Rainbow Cottage would do nicely. Mrs Green would be careful not to knock them down with her mop and duster. Otherwise the garden shed might do. There they would stay until the warm spring sunshine brought them out again, usually about April time.

Sam Snail was eating fit to bust, so that he would be good and strong to seal up the door of his shell and sleep the winter away, safe and secure in his wall.

And snug was what Sarah Slug wanted to be, snug as a bug in a rug! Though she would be snug as a slug under the roots of a rose bush. It was her usual winter home, and well protected against frost and snow. It was well furnished, so she could sit and dream about Summer Fairs, and being in charge of grand celebrations when everyone cheered her efficiency.

Winter was no problem for the ants; they had ample stores set by for emergencies, and Anthony had rigged up lots of interesting ways of storing food and moving it around. Whether they would work or not was another matter. Their home was a large one, with a maze of tunnels and chambers.

In the woodpile, the woodlice were making decisions about where to spend the winter months, because they always moved house in the autumn. Even though Mrs Green always checked the logs for animals before she burnt them, they didn't want to be caught napping in one of them. So they always moved house in good time, usually deep under the floorboards of the garden shed, but sometimes to the foundations of the cottage. At the moment, they were still undecided.

No one had seen Martin Millipede for a while, so it was thought that he had made his arrangements earlier this year.

And Wally Worm had lots of tunnels. Some went deep down into the ground so that he could escape the frosts, and some were near the surface so that he could pull in a few more rotting leaves on rainy days. This was his favourite food.

George Grasshopper was still singing his favourite songs around the garden, most of which began with rick-a-tick, or zick-a-zack. He really liked his new home, and autumn was one of his favourite times. He was such a happy grasshopper, and had become friendly with Lucy and Lenny Ladybird, so they might share winter quarters.

The garden was a lovely sight in autumn. There were so many lovely shades of colour everywhere, and Mrs Green was doing her best to tidy up the fallen leaves which Mr Bill had helped her put on the compost heap. It was a busy time for gardeners everywhere, and she had planted lots of bulbs for a colourful spring.

And although Mrs Green didn't know it, Sidney Spider was fed up with being bashed on the head by falling leaves, and was spending most of his time under the tiles of the kitchen roof, watching for the open kitchen door!

Also by Betty Salthouse
THE FOSSIL HUNTERS

When ten-year-old Jamie Rollings takes up fossil-hunting for a hobby, he stumbles across some exciting discoveries on the nearby estate that lead to new friendships and surprises that make this summer holiday truly special and unforgettable.

This traditional children's adventure story is set in an English country village in the days when children played outdoors with their friends all summer long. They seek their own entertainment and excitement in the real world instead of online, and the latest technology they have at their disposal is the fax machine!

Also by Betty Salthouse

CUCKOO CALL

Brains, the baby blackbird, thinks there's something odd about the huge new chick in the nest, but no-one else believes him. Can he save his family from disaster before it's too late? With the help of his new friend, Pij, the woodpigeon, he's determined to do his best.

This dramatic story about the survival of birds in the wild will appeal to any children who enjoy realistic stories about animals.

Also by Betty Salthouse

PARROT TALK

When nine-year-old Jamie Horton rescues a lost parrot and smuggles it into his bedroom, he has to act fast to learn how to care for it without revealing his secret to his bossy big sister and anxious mum. But then the bird escapes and Jamie fears the worst.

Will Jamie ever see Sidney again? One thing's for certain – Jamie's life will never be the same again.

A traditional English adventure story, ideal for children who love animals, especially parrots and birdlife.

Printed in Great Britain
by Amazon